GIRLS ROCK!

Bowling ... s

Holly Smith D...

illustrated by
Lloyd Foye

RISING ★ STARS

S/5143939

First published in Great Britain by
RISING STARS UK LTD 2005
76 Farnaby Road, Bromley, BR1 4BH

Reprinted 2006

For information visit our website at:
www.risingstars-uk.com

British Library Cataloguing in Publication Data

A CIP record for this book is available from the British Library.

ISBN: 1-905056-18-4

First published in 2005 by
MACMILLAN EDUCATION AUSTRALIA PTY LTD
627 Chapel Street, South Yarra, Australia 3141

Visit our website at www.macmillan.com.au

Associated companies and representatives throughout the world.

Series created by Felice Arena and Phil Kettle
Project Management by Limelight Press Pty Ltd
Cover and text design by Lore Foye
Illustrations by Lloyd Foye

Printed in Malaysia

GIRLS ROCK!
Contents

Ellie   *Rachel*

CHAPTER 1

Bully Boy

It's Friday night. Ellie and Rachel
are at the bowling alley. Ellie's dad
has just dropped them off. The girls
are waiting in the queue to hire
bowling shoes.

Ellie "What would happen if I
  dropped a bowling ball on your
  foot?"

Rachel "It's really noisy in here. Wow!
  It sounds like a thunderstorm. Can
  you hear that?"

Ellie (loudly) "Earth to Rachel, are you listening? What would happen if I dropped a bowling ball on your foot?"

Rachel "My foot would explode. I would scream and shout. And I might even die—is that a good enough answer?"

Ellie "No, more drama please!"

The girls get their shoes and walk
to their lane. Rachel puts her bottle
of water on the table. The girls put
on their bowling shoes.

Ellie "Now we have to choose our
  bowling balls. Come on. Over here."

Ellie leads Rachel over to a large rack where lots of bowling balls are stacked. The girls study the balls, occasionally picking one up to see how heavy it is.

Ellie "I'll take this one. I love blue—it looks like the Earth."

Rachel "This one's mine. Yellow, like the Sun."

As Rachel and Ellie carry the balls back to their lane, two boys from school start bowling in the lane next to them. While the girls are getting ready, the tall boy reaches over and grabs Rachel's water.

Ellie "He's got your drink, Rachel."

CHAPTER 2

Runaway Ball

Rachel looks up from her lane.

Rachel "Hey, that's mine!"

The boy tilts his head back, draining the bottle. His friend just watches and laughs.

Rachel (madder and louder) "What do you think you're doing? That's my water."

The boy totally ignores the girls. He puts the empty bottle back on the table and goes to choose another ball.

Rachel "I can't believe that. What a jerk! I hate bullies!"

Ellie "Yes, and he's top of the jerk list. Ignore him. Here, have some of mine. Come on, let's bowl. You go first. Remember, you get two throws each turn. I'll type in our names and the machine will keep score."

Ellie points to the electronic screen overhead where everyone's names and scores are displayed.

Rachel "I don't think I want everybody to see what a bad bowler I am. Leave my name out."

Ellie "I can't. Everyone who plays has to have their name there."

Rachel "I know, just don't use my real name. Today, my name is ... er ... Mary-Kate."

Ellie (laughing) "OK, cool. I'll be
  Ashley then."

Ellie enters "Mary-Kate" and
"Ashley" on the keyboard at the
scoring desk.

Meanwhile, a few women who are
talking loudly start to bowl in the
lane on the other side of the girls.

Rachel (whispering) "I've never seen a
lady with a tattoo like that before."
Ellie "My cousin had a tattoo on her
shoulder and my aunty went mad.
I thought it was cool."

Rachel gets up for her turn.

Rachel "Here goes nothing!"

She takes a few steps and gently tosses her ball towards the pins. The ball rolls about a metre then tumbles into the gutter. The boy in the next lane points and laughs.

Rachel "I'm hopeless. How
embarrassing!"
Ellie "It's OK. Just throw it harder
next time."

The return machine sends Rachel's
ball back to her. She picks up the
ball and throws it harder, but still
crooked. The ball jumps across the
gutter and lands in the lane where
the women are bowling.

Rachel "Oh, no, I'm such a loser!"

The woman with the tattoo walks over to the girls and asks if the yellow ball is Rachel's.

Rachel "Yes, thanks. Sorry, I got the wrong lane!"

CHAPTER 3

First Strike!

Rachel can't stop looking at the woman's tattoo.

Rachel "Who's Rocko?"

The woman looks puzzled until Rachel points at the tattoo. Smiling, the woman says Rocko is her old man.

Rachel "You mean your grandfather?"

The woman hands the ball back to Rachel and tells her that Rocko is her boyfriend.

Rachel "Oh, right. I thought you said it was the name of an old man."

Laughing, the woman then asks
Rachel if she'd like to learn to bowl
the ball correctly. Rachel nods. Side
by side, they go through the motions
of throwing the ball. Then Rachel rolls
her ball straight down the middle of
the lane and knocks down all ten pins
with a loud crash.

Ellie "Rachel, you got a strike! Way
  to go! That's really hard."
Rachel (turning to the woman)
  "Cool! Thanks for the tips."

As the woman leaves, she turns
to Rachel and says goodbye to
"Mary-Kate".

Rachel (laughing) "Great name,
  Mary-Kate! Hey *Ash-ley*, your
  turn."

Ellie (laughing) "Okay, *Mary-Kate*."

Rachel "I could get used to these
  names. They sound really cool."

Ellie (laughing) "Pity our parents
  didn't think of them earlier."

Just as Ellie is about to pick up her blue ball, the bully boy from the next lane grabs it and throws it down his lane. Ellie glares at him.

Ellie "I can't believe it!"

While Ellie's back is turned, a mouse crawls into one of her trainers.

CHAPTER 4

Bowling Backwards

Glaring at the boy, Ellie waits, arms crossed, for her ball to pop up on the return machine. When it does, she grabs it fast. The boy laughs.

Ellie (muttering) "Everything is
   sooooo funny."

Rachel "Can I show you how to
   throw the ball? Like that lady
   showed me?"

Ellie "No! I bowl all the time with
   my dad. I know how to do it."

Rachel "Hey, don't be mad at me. I
   didn't do anything."

Ellie grips her ball with her fingers and swings her right arm back. But, instead of swinging the ball forward, she drops it behind her—*boom!* The tall boy points and laughs again.

Rachel "Do you get points for bowling backwards?"

Ellie "I'm afraid not."

Rachel "It's still your turn."

The girls have a few more bowls but Ellie gets more and more frustrated.

Ellie "I'm sick of this. Let's go and play video games."

Rachel "Not yet. I'm just starting to get the hang of it."

Ellie "No, I'm going."

Ellie sits down on the bench, behind the scoring desk. She picks up her water, then reaches for her trainers to change back into. Rachel picks up her ball and is about to throw it when Ellie screams.

CHAPTER 5

Revenge by Accident

Ellie's scream echoes throughout the
bowling alley.

Ellie "AAAGGGHHHH!
AAAGGGHHHH!"

Ellie's water lands on the wooden floor, right where the bully boy is about to bowl. He slips on the wet floor and lands on his back. As he falls, the ball flies up in the air and lands right on his foot. He starts to scream.

Ellie "Well, well, well. The bully boy isn't so brave now!"

The bully boy's friend howls with laughter.

Rachel (shocked) "What happened to you, Ellie?"

Ellie "Tell you later. Let's go. Grab your trainers, but make sure to shake them first."

Looking confused, Rachel grabs
her trainers and follows Ellie to the
ladies' toilets. Once inside, they peek
through the half-open door to see
what's going on with the bully boy.

Rachel "What happened? Why did
you scream?"

Ellie "A mouse jumped out of my
shoe. It scared me, that's all. And
my water went everywhere.
Imagine a little bit of water causing
such a big fall?"
Rachel "Mmm, imagine."

The girls watch as the boy jumps
up and down, yelling something
about "Mary-Kate" and "Ashley."

Rachel (smiling) "Who are they?"
Ellie "Beats me!"

The girls dissolve into fits of
laughter.

Ellie "They're pretty cool bowlers,
whoever they are!"

GIRLS ROCK!
Bowling Lingo

Rachel

Ellie

ball return How you get your ball back after you throw it—it pops up on the return machine.

gutter ball What you call a ball if it rolls into the gutter before it reaches the pins.

lane The playing area you throw the ball down towards the set of pins.

pins The bottle-shaped objects you try to knock down with your bowling ball.

spare What you get when you knock down all ten pins with two throws.

strike What you get when you knock down all ten pins with one throw.

GIRLS ROCK!
Bowling Must-dos

☆ Wear clean socks if you go bowling so that no-one can complain about you having smelly feet while you change shoes.

☆ Think "straight" when you bowl— keep your back straight as you slide to release the ball, keep your arm straight as you release the ball, and slide straight forward.

☆ If you ever drop the ball behind you while taking your turn, just smile, say "oops" and try again.

☆ After you throw, wait until your ball comes back on the return machine.

☆ Never chase your ball down the lane.

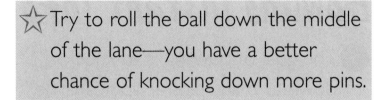

☆ Try to roll the ball down the middle of the lane—you have a better chance of knocking down more pins.

☆ Don't step across the start line when releasing your ball. If you do, you won't get any points for that throw— even if you knock all the pins down!

☆ If you can't stand the noise, take some earplugs to the bowling alley.

☆ Avoid hitting your ankle with the ball—it really hurts!

GIRLS ROCK!

Bowling Instant Info

- The goal of bowling is to knock down as many pins as you can. The more strikes you get, the easier it is.

- Bowling is one of the most popular sports in the world. In early times, it was often played outdoors. Today, bowling is mostly played inside.

- The highest score you can get for one game of bowling is 300— that's called a perfect game. It means that you get a strike every time it's your turn.

- English, Dutch and German settlers brought variations of bowling to the United States of America hundreds of years ago.

Archeologists have found evidence in tombs that ancient Egyptians had a game like bowling thousands of years ago.

The first machine to pick up pins and put them in place again (called a "pinsetter") was introduced in 1952 in Brooklyn, New York. Before that, "pin boys" were hired to pick up the pins and reset them. You were called a "pin boy" regardless of whether you were a girl or boy, young or old.

In 1998, a man named David Kremer won a world record with bowling balls. He stacked 10 bowling balls vertically, without using anything sticky to hold them together.

Think Tank

1 What do you call it when you knock down all 10 pins with one throw?

2 What kind of socks should you wear if you go bowling?

3 What do you call it when you knock down all 10 pins with two throws?

4 What do you call a ball that rolls into the gutter?

5 Which ancient civilisation was likely to have played a form of bowling?

6 How do you pick the right bowling ball?

7 What would you do if you find a mouse taking a nap inside your trainer?

8 Who invented the game of bowling?

Answers

1 If you knock down all 10 pins with one throw, it's called a strike.

2 If you go bowling, wear clean socks. That way, no-one can say you have smelly feet!

3 If you knock down all 10 pins with two throws, it's called a spare.

4 If your ball rolls into the gutter, it's called a gutter ball.

5 The Egyptians were likely to have played a form of bowling.

6 Pick the coolest looking ball—just make sure you can lift it so that you can throw it!

7 If you find a mouse taking a nap in your trainer, tap your shoe lightly on the floor and the mouse will hop out and run away!

8 No-one knows for sure who invented the game of bowling. Chances are that cavemen threw stones at piles of sticks, and they really invented bowling!

How did you score?

- If you got 8 answers correct, keep practising your game—you might even make a living as a professional bowler.

- If you got 6 answers correct, you can try to get a job as a "pin girl" at your local bowling alley.

- If you got fewer than 4 answers correct, think about learning to juggle bowling pins in the circus, rather than trying to knock them down with a ball!

Hey Girls!

I love to read and hope you do, too. The first book I really loved was called "Mary Poppins." It was full of magic (well before Harry Potter) and it got me hooked on reading. I went to the library every Saturday and left with a pile of books so heavy I could hardly carry them!

Here are some ideas about how you can make "Bowling Buddies" even more fun. At school, you and your friends can be actors and put on this story as a play. To bring the story to life, bring in some props from home such as a bottle of water, a stuffed mouse and a pair of trainers. Maybe you can set up a bowling alley somewhere at school.

Who will be Ellie? Who will be Rachel? Who will be the narrator? (That's the person who reads the parts between when Ellie or Rachel say something.) Once you've decided on these details, you're ready to act out the story in front of the class. I bet everyone will clap when you are finished! Hey, a talent scout from a television station might be watching.

See if someone at home will read this story out loud with you. Reading at home is important and a lot of fun as well.

Do you know what my dad used to tell me? "Readers are leaders".

And, remember, Girls Rock!

GIRLS ROCK!
When We Were Kids

Holly

Shey

Holly talked to Shey, another *Girls Rock!* author.

Holly "Where did you learn to bowl?"

Shey "My dad helped me. How did you learn?"

Holly "At school, in P. E. class, with plastic pins and a large rubber ball."

Shey "What do you like best about tenpin bowling?"

Holly "I like all those crashing sounds."

Shey "Are you a good bowler?"

Holly "Well, if they gave out prizes for the most gutter balls, I'd have a lot of trophies!"

GIRLS ROCK!
What a Laugh!

Q What kind of cats like to go bowling?

A Alley cats.

GIRLS ROCK!

Read about the fun
that girls have in these
GIRLS ROCK! titles:

The Sleepover

Pool Pals

Bowling Buddies

Girl Pirates

Netball Showdown

School Play Stars

Diary Disaster

Horsing Around

GIRLS ROCK! books are available from
most booksellers. For mail order information
please call Rising Stars on 01933 443862 or visit
www.risingstars-uk.com